Weathering the Storm

By Marybeth Wessels Misgen
Illustrations by Linda Bennefeld Niebling

Published 2013
ISBN 978-0-615-91668-2
P. Hanson Marketing, Inc.
1407 West 4th Street, Red Wing, Minnesota 55066
phmarketing@qwestoffice.net

One brilliant summer day a tiny sailboat came near the lighthouse. He was very small compared to the huge ships and yachts the lighthouse usually saw. He seemed curious, gentle, and innocent.

It was obvious the little boat hadn't experienced much in his life. Immediately there was a bond between the two like that of a mother and her newborn son.

The little boat had touched the heart of the lighthouse and made her feel alive. She felt compassion and opened herself to the magic of knowing the sailboat.

Day after day the lighthouse and boat were together. They were inseparable. The lighthouse was watchful, mindful of the tiny boat as it bobbled around the water. She loved to hear the boat gently gliding along the spurts of waves and to hear the sails flap quietly in the breeze.

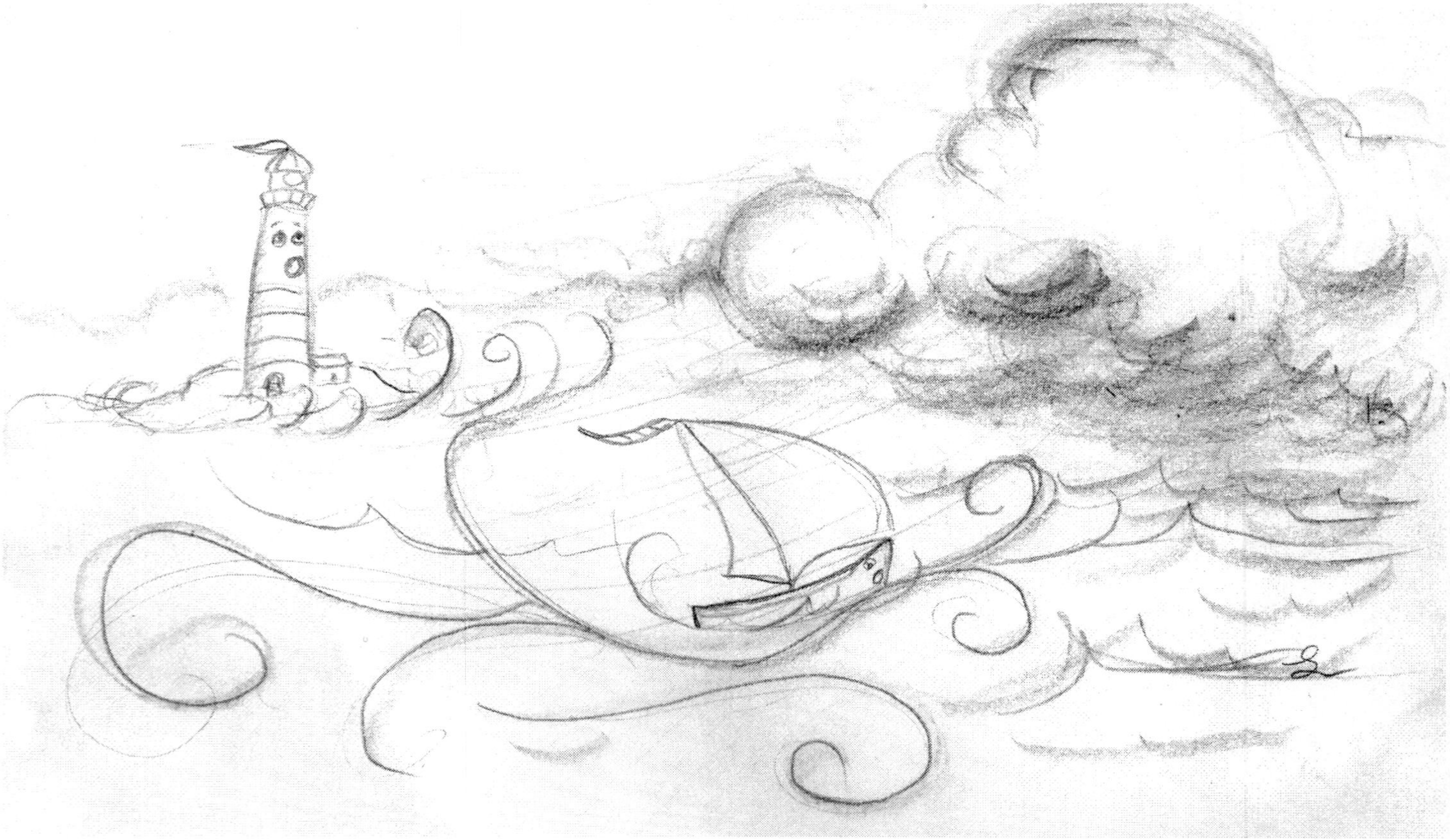

One warm, humid day the skies were deep gray and filled with mischief. The lighthouse sensed danger in the air and felt a sense of panic erupting within. She tried to call out to the sailboat, but it was much too late!

The miniature boat was plummeting helplessly up and down in the wickedly monstrous waves. The lighthouse watched in pain as the boat struggled to stay afloat. A tiny tear trickled down the lighthouse.

It was far too painful to watch the boat fight for life. She forced herself to watch in an effort to offer support, compassion, and a deeply rooted love. Suddenly, the single tear turned into a flood of tears gushing from the lighthouse. She tried to be strong as the sail was shredded in the gnashing wind. She felt helpless and alone as she continued to ask herself, "WHY?"

The storm lasted for what seemed an eternity. The lighthouse and sailboat struggled to ease each other's pain as the black, stormy days continued.

Finally, the storm cleared. The waters became manageable, then glassy and clear. Slowly, the wind died down until all was calm again. The sun came out and rays of warmth spread all around, though the warmth the sailboat and lighthouse felt came from within.